THIS

READ with ME ™

BOOK
BELONGS TO

_____

Library of Congress Cataloging in Publication Data

Perle, Ruth Lerner.
   Cinderella with Benjy and Bubbles.

   (Read With Me series)
   Based on Cendrillon, by C. Perrault.
   SUMMARY: A rhymed retelling of the classic
tale with Benjy the bunny and Bubbles the cat
clarifying values as the story unfolds.
   [1. Stories in rhyme. 2. Fairy tales.
3. Folklore—France] I. Razzi, James.
II. Perrault, Charles, 1628-1703. Cendrillon.
III. Title. IV. Series.
PZ8.3.P423Ci   [398.2]   [E]   77-27870
ISBN 0-03-040236-0

Cinderella
with Benjy and Bubbles

Adapted by RUTH LERNER PERLE

Illustrated by JIM RAZZI

Holt, Rinehart and Winston • New York

This story happened long ago;
Benjy, the bunny, says it was so.

Poor Cinderella, in patches and grime
Had step-sisters who were mean all the time.
To add to Cinderella's troubles,
They had a naughty cat named Bubbles.

Cinderella, with pail and broom,
Cleaned and dusted every room.
The step-sisters just sat and ate,
And Bubbles, the cat, thought that was great.

Cinderella was sweet and kind.
Her step-sisters were mean to her.

One day, a messenger came to call.
He announced, "The Prince will have a ball!
Tomorrow night, come one, come all!
Gather in the palace hall!"

All the young girls were invited;
All the grown-ups were excited.

The sisters shrieked, "This is our chance!
We will go to the Prince's dance.
He is in the prime of life;
One of us should be his wife!"

The Prince was having a dance.

The sisters chose their finest clothes;
They gathered fancy hose and bows
While Cinderella sewed and pressed
And helped her step-sisters get dressed.

When Cinderella's work was through,
She shyly asked, "May I go, too?"
The sisters laughed and screamed, "Not you!
You're ragged and torn from collar to shoe!"

They went off without a care,
Leaving Cinderella there.
Benjy, the bunny, tried for a while
To comfort her and make her smile.
But no matter how the bunny tried,
Cinderella sighed and cried.

The step-sisters did not let Cinderella
go to the dance.
"How I wish I could go!" she cried.

Then, all of a sudden she looked up and listened!
Something outside had tinkled and glistened!
Out in the garden, in the moonlight,
Stood a kind fairy who glowed in the night!
"I'm your godmother," the good fairy said,
Placing her wand on the young girl's head.
Whoosh! In a shining, golden cloud,
Stood Cinderella, tall and proud.
Her slippers were glass, her gown was blue;
Her dearest wish was coming true.

The story is no longer tragic!
The friendly fairy with her magic
Turned a pumpkin into a coach
Using her *one-two-three* approach!
Once more she called out, "Once, twice, thrice!"
And pointed her wand at six grey mice.

"I think," meowed Bubbles, "I'm getting thinner,
I'll make those six grey mice my dinner!"

A kind fairy gave Cinderella glass slippers
and a dress. She gave her a coach, too.
The fairy said, "You may go to the dance."

Bubbles went after the mice, of course,
But each grey mouse became a horse!
And the fairy wasn't finished yet.
She pointed at Cinderella's pet.
He became coachman in a high seat
And said, "Good fairy, that trick is neat!"

"My magic ends!" the fairy said,
"*At midnight you must be in bed!*"

The fairy said, "You must be home by midnight." Cinderella said, "I will leave the dance on time."

Cinderella, at the ball,
Was the fairest one of all.

The people asked, "Who can she be?"
The Prince said, "Will you dance with me?"

The Prince asked Cinderella to dance.
"Who are you?" he asked.

They danced and danced and danced.

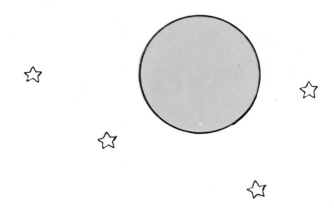

Then Cinderella heard the clock.
It went, "Tick-tock, tick-tock, tick-tock."
She looked at its face, and trembling with fright,
She saw that the time was almost midnight!

It was time for Cinderella to go home.

The clock was clanging, two, three, four
As Cinderella rushed to the door.
She ran down the stairs, two steps by two
And in her hurry, lost her shoe!

There, on the step, woe and alas,
Was the slipper, made of glass.
But Cinderella could not stop
To go back and pick it up.

Cinderella ran down the steps.
She lost one glass slipper.

The Prince ran out into the night,
But Cinderella was out of sight.
When he looked by the palace stair,
Just a pumpkin, six mice, and a rabbit were there.
Then, as he searched and looked and listened,
He noticed a slipper that sparkled and glistened.

The Prince held the slipper in his hand
And decided to search throughout the land
To find the foot that fit the shoe.
He told his court what he would do:
"The girl whose foot can fit inside,
I will ask to be my bride!"

The Prince picked up the slipper.
"I want to marry the girl who can wear
this slipper," he said.

All the day, throughout the town,
The Prince walked up, the footman, down.
Not even one girl's foot would fit—
And the Prince was getting tired of it.

In the last house, the step-sisters waited.
They winked, they curtsied, they undulated!
The Prince stood quietly at the door;
The footman set the shoe on the floor.

First, the shorter sister tried,
But her foot was much too wide.
The taller sister's foot was wrong;
Her toes and heels were far too long.
No matter how they forced the shoe,
Neither sister's foot would do.

The slipper did not fit the step-sisters.

The Prince was about to leave the house
When he noticed a bunny at play with a mouse.
He watched as they hopped to the fireplace
And there, he saw a sweet girl's face!
"Bring the slipper at once!" he cried.
"Here is someone who has not tried!"

The step-sisters were a funny sight
When Cinderella's foot fit right.

The Prince embraced Cinderella and said,
"You are the one I would like to wed."
"Oh, Prince," was her answer, "I've thought much about it.
I've kept it a secret, but now I can shout it!
I'll marry you gladly and be a princess
And leave my step-sisters and all of the mess!"

"How lovely!" sighed Benjy, "Oh, I am so glad!"
"How awful!" cried Bubbles, "Oh, I am so mad!"

Cinderella tried the slipper. It fit!
The Prince said, "Cinderella, be my bride."
Cinderella said, "Yes."

All the people in the town
Wore their finest suit or gown.
They all came to the royal marriage
By foot or boat or horse-drawn carriage.
The butchers and the bakers, too,
And the keepers of the zoo,
The doctors, lawyers and the teachers,
The candy-makers and the preachers,
The circus clowns and the lamplighters,
The poets, actors and the fighters.
Bubbles and Benjy and the step-sisters, too,
Walked together two-by-two.

Everybody came to the wedding.

No one had ever seen such a feast!
There were treats from the North and South and East.
There were cookies and cream puffs and gumdrops, too,
And crackers that probably came from the zoo.

In the middle of the splendid room
Stood Cinderella and her groom.
With joy and love and gentle laughter
They lived together ever after.

Cinderella and the Prince were married.

THE END